This book belongs to:

For Nathaniel – GD
For Mum, Dad and Michelle – AB

With special thanks (and apologies) to The Clash,
whose song London Calling inspired the title of this book.
(In turn The Clash's title London Calling came from the BBC World Service's
radio station identification: 'This is London calling...' used during World War II).

And Dr. Seuss, who inspired verse five, but as far as the author knows,
never actually visited London....

This edition published 2017 by order of the Tate Trustees by Tate Publishing,
a division of Tate Enterprises Ltd, Millbank, London SW1P 4RG
www.tate.org.uk/publishing

First published in hardback 2014
This edition published 2017

Text © Gabby Dawnay 2014. Illustrations © Alex Barrow 2014
Artwork by Paul Noble © Paul Noble 2014

A catalogue record for this book is available from the British Library
ISBN 978-1-84976-517-6

Distributed in the United States and Canada by ABRAMS, New York
Library of Congress Control Number applied for
Colour reproduction by Evergreen Colour Management Ltd, Hong Kong
Printed in China by Toppan Leefung Printing Ltd

LONDON CALLS!

GABBY DAWNAY   ALEX BARROW

Tate Publishing

Big Ben is chiming; it's quarter to eight and

We jump on a bus where an oyster's the fare

VISIT

THE CROWN JEWE

and over the river to Parliament Square!

Marble
Arch
159

There are statues of lions and palaces fine;

there are parks packed with trees,

fancy restaurants to dine...

There's the Southbank, the Tates,

either Modern or Brit,

showing

new art

and old art and

benches to sit...

There are shops selling shoes, there are shops selling socks, there are shops selling fashionable dresses and clocks...

You can zoom on the tube, you can bicycle, scoot

You can talk as you walk, while the motorcars hoot!

There is concrete, graffiti and tower blocks high...

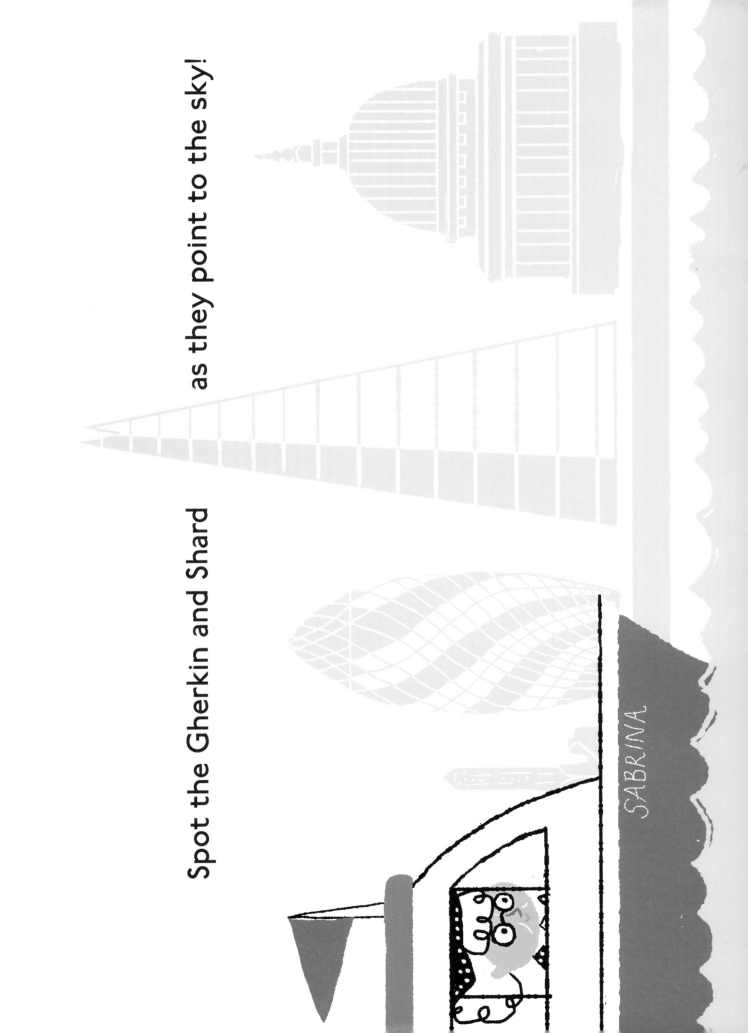

Spot the Gherkin and Shard
as they point to the sky!

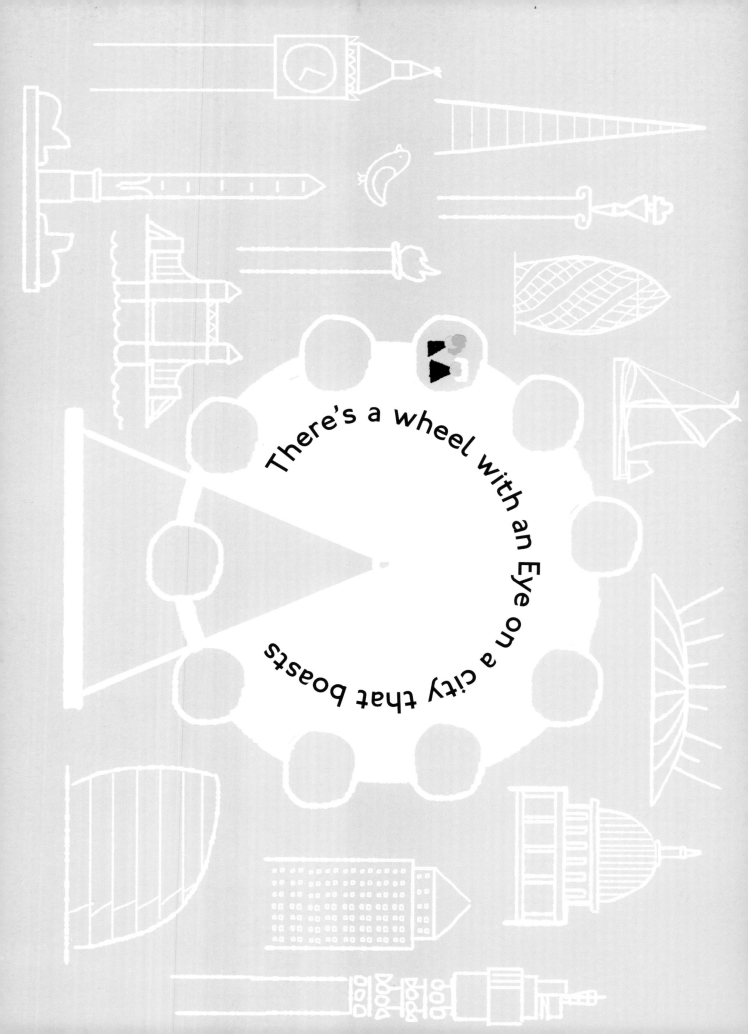

There's a wheel with an Eye on a city that boasts

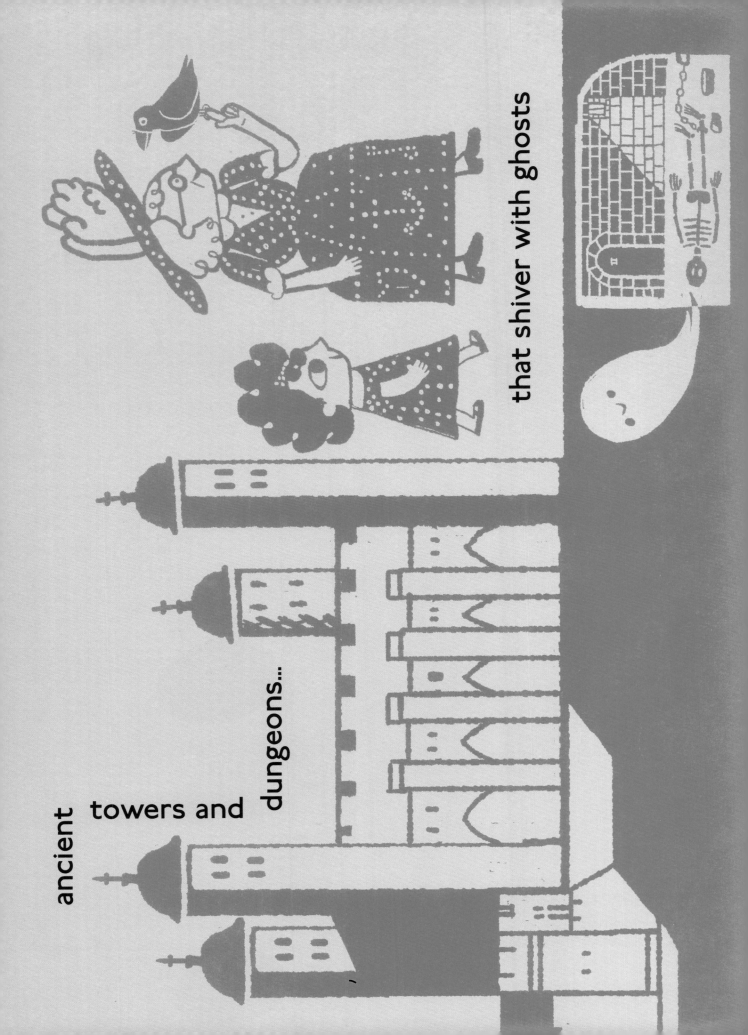

ancient towers and dungeons...

that shiver with ghosts

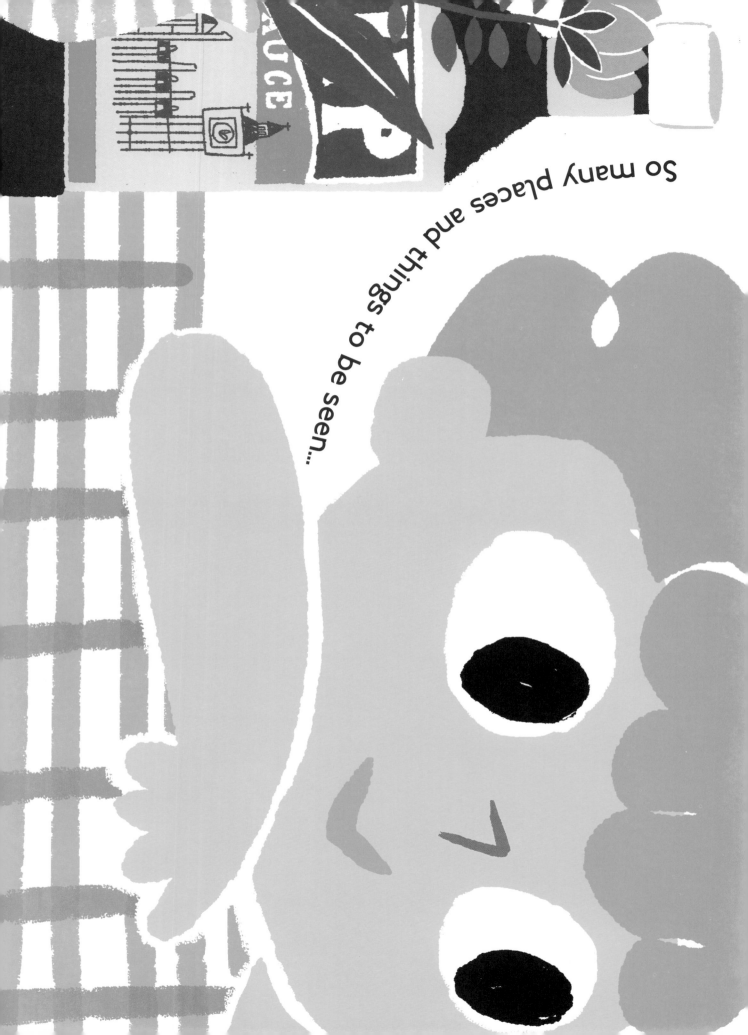

So many places and things to be seen...

from the column of Nelson to tea with the Queen...

You'll find theatres
and cinemas, markets
and stalls

...next London calls. Oh you'd better listen when

Big Ben is chiming; it's quarter to eight

and supper is ready – we mustn't be late!

Meet Granny Rose and little Pearl

Hello! My name's Pearl and this is my Granny Rose. We're known as 'Pearlies' because our clothes are covered in pearl buttons!

Pearlies raise money for all sorts of good causes.

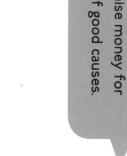

There are lots of funny names for buildings in London like The Gherkin, The Shard, Big Ben and The London Eye.

Thanks for coming on our whistle-stop tour of London – hope you enjoyed it! London is full of fantastic people and amazing places – there's so much to explore. Here are a few other things I bet you didn't know about this big, old, awesome city of ours. Over to you, Gran!

Can you spot them all in the pictures?

Did you know the saying 'The world is my oyster' comes from a play by William Shakespeare?

Is that why London travel cards are called Oysters?

Yes! I do love an oyster with a dash of Tabasco sauce. Scrummy! But they're pricey nowadays, mind... back in Shakespeare's day, oysters were as cheap as chips!

Was that back when you were a girl, Gran?

Steady on, Pearl, I'm not THAT old....

How many types of London transport can you spot in the book?

It's the Albert Bridge – one of the many bridges over the Thames. There are about 214 ways of crossing the river from start to finish, including all the big London bridges, the railway bridges, foot bridges and tunnels. That's a crossing for every mile!

That's mean! I love the statues all over London. Especially the Boy with a Dolphin, near my favourite bridge called... Gran, what's my favourite bridge called?

They did. Eight years. Poor old Edwin Landseer (he was the famous artist that made them) they took him so long to finish that everyone made fun of him.

Look at those lions, Pearl! Four bronze beasts at the bottom of Nelson's Column.

They must've taken ages to make – they're massive!

It is Pearl, it's the longest river in England. Londoners used to call it Old Father Thames because, I suppose, it's such a long, old river running through the heart of London.

I'm not surprised! There are over 1,000 green spaces in London; not just parks, commons, heaths and public gardens, but garden squares, woods, city farms and cemeteries.

Do you have a favourite London park?

Did you know that seen from above, more than half of London is green or blue?

Wow! So the Thames is...214 miles long?!

There's Buckingham Palace!
The Queen has garden parties there, doesn't she?

Yes, I've been to tea at the Palace.

Tea with the Queen?! What did you eat, Gran?

Oh it was lovely, although I seem to remember the sandwiches being a bit on the small side. Let's see, we had...

I like a good jellied eel!

Delicious!
What's your favourite food ever, Gran?

Yuck! I like chips with loads of vinegar!
Do you think the Queen likes chips, Gran?

Come on Pearl,
let's go home for tea.

Can you spot Buckingham Palace
in the book?

Buckingham Palace
TEATIME MENU

Earl Grey tea

accompanied by...
Honey and cream sponge cake
Chocolate biscuit cake
(Prince William's favourite)

Cucumber sandwiches
Smoked salmon sandwiches
(all crustless)

Jam pennies
*(tiny raspberry jam sandwiches cut into
circles the size of an old English penny)*

Why's it called the tube?

Shall we get on the tube?

Oh I see! I like the whoosh of wind through the tunnel just before the train arrives – it's warm and stinky!

Because of the shape of the underground tunnels.

The tube is very old, too – the first bit was built 150 years ago. It's the oldest underground railway in the world!

London is a very old city, isn't it Gran?

Yes, it is – but it's still growing and changing. It keeps me young, just like you do.